W9-CII-452

JESS & JAYLEN

TROUBLE WITH CHEATING

BY BLAKE HOENA • ILLUSTRATED BY DANA REGAN

Published by The Child's World®
1980 Lookout Drive • Mankato, MN 56003-1705
800-599-READ • www.childsworld.com

Acknowledgments
The Child's World®: Mary Berendes, Publishing Director
The Design Lab: Design
Red Line Editorial: Editorial direction and production

ISBN 9781631434426
LCCN 2014930638

Printed in the United States of America
Mankato, MN
July, 2014
PA02215

TABLE OF CONTENTS

FRACTIONS

Jess wanted to scream. For her math homework, she was working on fractions. They were the worst. Sure, she could tell the difference between 1/2 and 1/3. That was easy. But 2/3 and 3/4? Or worse, 3/7 and 2/5? Impossible.

"GAHHHH!" she screamed.

She wanted to scribble out all the problems in her math book. Instead, she slammed it shut.

"GAHHHH!" she screamed again, slapping her pencil down on her desk.

Just then, her bedroom door creaked open. Her mom peeked in.

"Is everything OK, honey?" she asked.

"No!" Jess shot back.

Jess hated it when her mom called her "honey." It made her feel like a baby. She was in third grade, not kindergarten.

"I made you a smoothie," her mom said. She set down a glass filled with a thick, green liquid on Jess's desk.

"Mom, it's green," Jess complained. Green smoothies were dangerous.

"I didn't put anything weird in it," her mom said.

"No pickle juice?" Jess asked.

"No pickle juice," her mom answered. "No seaweed or spinach either. Just yogurt, an apple, and brussels sprouts for texture."

"Ew, brussels sprouts!" Jess groaned, scrunching up her nose. She pushed the smoothie away.

"I'm only kidding," her mom said. "It's green because I put kiwi in it."

Jess thought about asking her mom for help with her math, but she had done that once before. It was a huge mistake. Her mom kept saying, "That's not how I was taught to do it when I was your age." By the time they were done, Jess was more confused than ever. She even failed her next quiz.

"Don't stay up too late," Jess's mom said, shutting the door behind her.

If Jess failed another quiz, her teacher would send a note home to her mom.

And her mom would be mad. That would mean lost privileges. No skateboarding on Saturdays. No hanging out with friends on weeknights. No Jake's Pizza for Friday dinners.

Jess couldn't handle that.

She decided to call Jaylen. He was a math whiz. He was also her best friend. He lived just down the block, and they had known each other practically forever.

"Hey, Jaylen," Jess said when her friend picked up the phone. "How're you doing with that math homework?"

"Done. It was simple," he said. "Fighting zombies now."

Nuts, Jess thought. Jaylen was obsessed with video games. He wouldn't want to work on homework with her if he was gaming. And she didn't really want to ask for help anyway. Jaylen could get pretty snotty

about things like math and chess and video games. He might think she was dumb or something.

So instead she asked, "Do we have a math quiz tomorrow?"

"Yup," Jaylen replied. "TAKE THAT, you brain-eating zombie!" The sound of an explosion echoed over the phone.

Jess could tell her friend was distracted. She didn't want to bother him. But what was she going to do?

CHAPTER TWO

SNEAK A PEEK

The next morning, Jaylen waited at the bus stop. He checked his watch. Jess was late. No surprise there. She was always late.

When the bus rolled to a stop, Jaylen glanced over at his friend's apartment building. No Jess.

Jaylen climbed on the bus and took a seat. Then he pulled out a folder from his backpack. He had drawn two columns on it. One marked the times Jess caught the bus. The other showed the times she missed it. He kept track just to mess with her.

The bus lurched forward. Jaylen looked out his window. Still no Jess. Time to mark another one in the "miss" column.

At school, Jaylen took his seat in the front of the class. Jess didn't arrive until just before the bell rang. She plopped down next to him.

"You missed the school bus today," Jaylen said. He held up his notebook with the marks on it.

"I know," Jess growled. "Don't mess with me today, OK?"

They sat quietly as Mrs. Johnson, their teacher, read the daily announcements. Then they broke into reading groups. Jaylen didn't have a chance to ask Jess why she was so cranky until lunch.

They sat with their friends Tou and Tanya. But Jess wasn't saying anything. She was just moving her food around with her fork.

"What's up with you today?" Jaylen asked Jess.

Jess kept staring down at her lunch.

"Just tired," she said. "I stayed up late studying for our math quiz."

"It's only fractions," Jaylen replied. "Super simple."

"Yeah, nothing to worry about," Tou added.

They don't get it, Jess thought. *It's not easy for everyone.*

She didn't say another word during lunch. She just focused on her food:

something yellow and gooey with noodles, green beans, and mushy cantaloupe.

Almost as horrible as one of Mom's smoothies, Jess thought.

After lunch, Jess and Jaylen headed back to class. For math, they were divided up into different sections. Jess and Jaylen stayed with Mrs. Johnson. But some of their classmates went to other sections. They changed up their seating assignments as students from other classes joined Mrs. Johnson's math section. Jess took a seat behind Jaylen.

"OK, class," Mrs. Johnson said with a smile.

Mrs. Johnson always smiled. Jaylen said it was because she was a robot. She was programmed to smile to look human. Jess wasn't so sure. But it was weird how Mrs. Johnson never stopped smiling. And it didn't matter if you turned in your homework or not. Whether you passed or failed a test. She always smiled the same smile.

"It's time for a quiz on fractions," said Mrs. Johnson as she held up a stack of papers. "You'll have 15 minutes to complete 20 questions."

After handing out the quizzes, she added, "Good luck!"

Jess stared down at her paper. The questions looked like gobbledygook. Just a bunch of numbers and slashes.

In front of her, Jaylen was madly scribbling away.

The first question read, "Which is >: 2/3 or 5/8?" Jess thought it was 5/8. Five was greater than two. But she wasn't sure that was correct, and she didn't want to get the first question wrong. So she leaned forward to check her answer against Jaylen's. He had

circled "2/3." She scribbled out her answer and changed it.

Another question read, "If Sue collects 15 eggs and 2/5 of them are brown, how many brown eggs does she find?"

Jess stared at the question for a moment. Again, she wasn't sure. Five went into fifteen three times.

Three's the answer, she thought, *but better check it against Jaylen's.*

Jess craned her head so she could see over Jaylen's shoulder. He had written down "6."

How did he get that? Jess wondered. Oh, well. She wrote down "6."

Instead of reading the next question, Jess thought it would be easier to see what Jaylen got for an answer first. Then she could see if she was able to figure it out herself. She glanced around the classroom to make sure no one was watching. The other students were busy working on their quizzes. Mrs. Johnson was at her desk reading something and smiling.

Jess leaned forward to peek over Jaylen's shoulder. He must have sensed something. Just then, he glanced back at her.

CHAPTER THREE

JAYLEN'S NEW TRICK

"What?" Jaylen whispered.

"What did you get for the third question?" Jess whispered back.

He looked confused.

Then to her surprise, Jaylen pushed his quiz to the edge of his desk. She could see his answer.

For "4/9 = ?/36," Jaylen had written "16." Jess copied it down.

After that, Jess thought she knew a few of the answers on her own. But mostly she relied on looking at Jaylen's quiz.

She ended up getting 16 out of 20. Jaylen got a perfect score.

Jess felt good about doing well on her quiz. That is, until Jaylen plopped down next to her on the bus ride home.

"Don't ever do that again," he said.

"Do what?" she asked.

"Cheat," he said. "You were copying my answers."

"But you let me," she shot back.

"I won't next time," he said. "I could get in trouble."

"So?"

"So?"

They both huffed and crossed their arms in front of them. They didn't say another word to each other until they were about to get off the bus.

"Hitting the skate park tomorrow?" Jess asked, staring straight ahead.

"Yeah," Jaylen said, without looking at her.

They were still mad at each other, but skateboarding was too important to miss. Nearly every weekend, they headed down to Washington Park. It was a big city park that had a skate park. Saturday mornings were reserved for junior skateboarders like

Jess and Jaylen. And they weren't going
to let a little disagreement keep them
from going.

―――――

The next morning, Jess stood on the deck
of the skate park's bowl. She watched Jaylen
as he tried to drop in. He leaned forward and
shot down the side of the bowl.

Every time he got to the bottom, he
stumbled backward and fell. His elbow pads
thunked loudly on the concrete.

He looked up at Jess.

"Can you show me how to drop in
again?" he asked.

"Sure," she said.

Jess balanced her board on top of the lip
of the bowl. Then she leaned forward. She
shot down the into the bowl. At the bottom,
she swiveled her hips so the board stayed
directly underneath her. She skated up the

opposite side of the bowl. She rolled to fakie, with the tail of her board now pointing forward. Then she stopped at the bottom.

"Just like that," she said to Jaylen.

Jaylen tried it again. He got to the bottom of the bowl and fell again.

"You gotta keep your board deck between your hips and the pavement at all times," Jess explained.

Jaylen gave it another go. This time he was a little wobbly, but he managed to stay on his board.

"You got it!" Jess said, high-fiving her friend.

On the bus ride back home, Jess asked Jaylen what he was doing the rest of the weekend.

"Probably blasting robots," Jaylen replied. One of his favorite video games was *Ragin' Robots*. "You?"

"I don't know," she said. "Got all your homework done?"

"Yeah," he said.

"Even math?" she asked.

He nodded.

What Jess really wanted to do was ask Jaylen for help with fractions. She still didn't understand them. But Jaylen had said they were super simple. She didn't want him to think that she couldn't do them. She didn't want her best friend to think she was dumb.

ANOTHER QUIZ

Monday, Jess stood in front of a smiling Mrs. Johnson. Her teacher held Jess's unfinished math homework in one hand.

"Jess, I don't understand it," Mrs. Johnson said. "You did so well on last week's quiz. But you haven't completed any of your math homework lately."

Jess just shrugged her shoulders.

"Is something wrong?" Mrs. Johnson asked. "Is everything OK at home?"

Jess's parents had gotten divorced a few years ago. Ever since then, teachers were always asking if things were OK at home. Jess knew they meant well. But it was getting annoying. If something was wrong

at home, Jess would say so. She was just
having trouble with fractions. No big deal.

"I'm fine," Jess said.

Jess wasn't sure Mrs. Johnson was
convinced. But her teacher didn't have any
more questions for her.

"Well, if you turn in any more incomplete homework, I'll have to send a note home to your mom," Mrs. Johnson warned.

Great, Jess thought. *Just great.*

That night at home, Jess called Jaylen. She had her math book open in front of her.

"What did you get for the first answer?" she asked Jaylen.

"5/9," he said.

"Me too," Jess lied. "What about question two?"

She got about half the answers out of Jaylen before he figured out what she was doing.

"Are you copying my homework?" he asked.

"No!" Jess lied again. "I just wanted to make sure I was getting things right."

Jaylen didn't buy it.

"Well, I gotta go," he said. He sounded mad. "I'm in the middle of ridding the world of zombie pirates."

Jess finished the rest of her homework on her own. But she wasn't very confident in the answers she came up with. At least Mrs. Johnson couldn't say anything about the homework not being done.

At school the next day, Mrs. Johnson said the two words that Jess hated the most: *pop quiz*. It was almost as if she knew Jess was struggling with fractions.

Everyone in class groaned. Everyone except for Jaylen, that is. He looked at pop quizzes like they were monsters in a video game. You went in knowing you'd have to face them. They could pop up anytime and anywhere. The key was being prepared.

This quiz was a real monster. Jess was stumped by the first question.

"2/3 + 2/3 = ?"

4/6, she thought.

But to be sure, she leaned forward to look at Jaylen's answer. He had written "4/3."

Why didn't he add the bottom numbers? Jess wondered. She wrote down "4/3" anyway.

Jaylen was already done with question two. Jess copied that one down, too.

She was waiting for him to finish with question three when he looked over his shoulder and caught her.

"Don't!" he mouthed at her.

"What?" she mouthed back.

"Don't look at my answers!" he hissed. Then he covered up his quiz with one arm.

"Hey!" she said out loud.

"Jess. Jaylen. Is something wrong?" Mrs. Johnson asked, smiling.

They both turned to face her.

Jaylen gulped. "No," he said.

"No," Jess said, quickly looking down at her quiz.

She hoped Mrs. Johnson wouldn't suspect anything. But it was hard to tell. She just smiled at them.

Jaylen didn't talk to Jess for the rest of the day. Even worse, he didn't sit with her on the bus. He found a seat toward the back and just stared out the window.

Once they got off, Jess stopped him and asked, "What's wrong?"

"You nearly got me in trouble," he said. "That's what."

"I would have gotten in trouble, too!" Jess shouted back.

"So?"

"So?"

Jess wasn't quite sure why she was shouting. Or why she was so mad. But she didn't want to talk to Jaylen anymore. He must have felt the same. Jaylen stomped off to his apartment building.

TUTOR

That night, Jess was worried about something other than fractions for a change. She was worried about her friendship with Jaylen. Sure, she knew she shouldn't cheat. She knew it was wrong. But what choice did she have? It was either cheat or fail.

I don't want anyone to think I'm dumb, she thought.

Why didn't Jaylen understand that? He was good at math and computers. Her thing was sports.

The next morning, Jess purposely missed the school bus. That meant she had to ride the city bus to Emerson Elementary. It took her a little longer to get to school. She arrived just before the bell rang.

"Hey," she said as she plopped down next to Jaylen.

"Hey," he replied.

Neither of them felt like saying much. They were both still mad at each other.

The bell rang. Mrs. Johnson read the daily announcements. Jess and Jaylen didn't talk to each other all morning. They were busy with school stuff until lunch.

As they ate, they hardly looked at each other. Jess talked to Tanya about a movie they had watched. Jaylen talked to Tou about learning how to drop into the bowl at the skate park.

"That's cool," Tou said. "I can roll in on the ramps. But they aren't as scary as the bowl. How'd you get the hang of that?"

"It's pretty steep," Jaylen said. "But Jess showed me how. She's nailed it."

Just then, Jess and Jaylen glanced at each other. Their eyes met for a second. Jess wasn't exactly sure what Jaylen was thinking. But he had just said something nice about her. That made her feel bad about missing the bus this morning so she wouldn't have to talk to him.

During their math section, Jess took her normal seat. The weird thing was that Jaylen wasn't in his.

That worried her.

Mrs. Johnson started by handing back their last quiz.

"Sorry I didn't get these back to you sooner," she explained with a smile. "But I had a little problem grading a couple of them."

Mrs. Johnson set Jess's quiz upside down on her desk. Jess flipped it over. Instead of a score on her test, there was a note that read, "See me after class."

Jess couldn't concentrate for the rest of class.

Does Mrs. Johnson know I cheated? Did she see me copy off Jaylen's test? Am I in trouble? Is he in trouble? Where is he? The thoughts raced through her head.

Finally, everyone got up to move to their seats for social studies. Jess walked up to Mrs. Johnson's desk. She held her test out in front of her.

"You wanted to talk to me?" Jess asked.

Mrs. Johnson sighed, and for once, she didn't smile.

Oh no, Jess worried. This had to be serious.

"Jess, you're a good student," Mrs. Johnson began. "Which is why I'm struggling to understand this. But can you explain why you did so well on one quiz, yet you failed this one? They both asked the same basic questions."

Jess looked down at her feet. She wasn't sure what to do. She would be in trouble if she told the truth. But could she really lie to Mrs. Johnson?

That would be worse than cheating, she thought.

Jess said nothing.

"How about this," Mrs. Johnson said. "Just tell me whether you were copying off Jaylen's quiz yesterday."

Jess kept looking down. She didn't want Mrs. Johnson to see the tears welling up in her eyes. But she nodded her head.

"I will have to send a note home to your mom," Mrs. Johnson said. "But you have a choice about what that note says."

That got Jess's attention. She looked up, not sure what her teacher was saying.

"I can send a note home saying that you cheated," Mrs. Johnson explained.

Jess felt her stomach sinking. Cheating! She couldn't imagine how angry her mom would be.

"Or I can say that you failed two quizzes," Mrs. Johnson continued, "and that you will need to retake them. But before you do, I'm going to assign you a tutor."

"What?" Jess was confused.

"We ask all students in advanced math to help other students," Mrs. Johnson said.

"Does this mean I'm being put in a lower section?" Jess asked.

"No, no, you're staying in my class," Mrs. Johnson said. "You just seem to be having trouble with what we're currently working on."

Just then, Jaylen walked in.

"Hey," he said with a wave.

Jess wanted to ask where he had been, but Mrs. Johnson answered that question for her.

"Jaylen's been moved up to advanced math," she said. "And I've asked him to be your tutor."

What? was all Jess could think.

CHAPTER SIX

PIZZA

Instead of riding the school bus home, Jess took the city bus. That way she could avoid Jaylen. Needing a tutor made Jess feel like she wasn't smart or something. Having Jaylen be her tutor was even worse. He must think she was a total dummy.

At first, her mom was upset to hear that Jess had failed two quizzes. But after she read Mrs. Johnson's note about Jess being assigned a tutor, her mom calmed down a bit.

Just before dinner, there was a knock on the door.

"It's for you!" Jess's mom called out.

Jess went to the door. There were actually
several people there to see her. Jaylen, his
older brother, Jack, and their younger
sister, Jenny.

"Hi, Jess," Jenny said.

"Hey," Jess said back. "What's up? Why
are you all here?"

"My dad's working a late shift at the
hospital," Jaylen said.

"So I'm taking the rug rats out for pizza,"
Jack added.

"We're going to Jake's!" Jenny chimed in excitedly.

Jake's Pizza was Jess and Jaylen's favorite restaurant. They went there whenever they got a chance.

"Want to come with us?" Jaylen asked.

Jess's mom was listening in on the conversation.

"Go ahead, honey," she said. "Unless you want to stay for some of my mystery meatloaf."

That did not sound safe. And Jess never said no to Jake's.

At the restaurant, each of them ordered a personal pizza. Then they went to sit down. Jaylen stayed at the counter to talk to the cook before joining them at their table.

What is he up to? Jess wondered.

When their pizzas arrived, Jess was surprised to see that each one was cut differently.

"Cool!" Jenny said. "Mine's cut into tiny pieces."

"What's this?" Jack asked.

"It's a math lesson for Jess," Jaylen explained.

"What?" Jess asked. She was confused.

"Come on, Jess," Jaylen explained. "You help me with everything, from how to shoot free throws to catching fly balls. Last week, you taught me how to drop in at the skate park."

Jess flushed. She knew he was right. Every time he struggled with some sporting activity, he asked for her help. She didn't think that made him bad at sports.

"I just wished you had asked me for help right away," he added.

"Even if you're in the middle of zapping zombies?" she asked.

"Sure," he said.

Then he pointed to everyone's pizzas.

"Now, for your first lesson, I had Jenny's pizza cut into ten wedges. Yours into eight. Mine into six. And Jack's into four."

"Is this gonna take long?" Jack asked. "I'm starving."

"Go ahead," Jaylen said. "Because I want Jess to see who has the most pizza left after everyone eats one slice."

They all grabbed a slice of their pizza and started eating.

Jess wasn't quite sure why, but pizza made talking about fractions more fun—especially Jake's special quadruple-cheese pizza.

NOW IT'S YOUR TURN!

1. Have you ever been tempted to cheat on a homework assignment? Why or why not? What did you do?

2. Jess struggles with fractions while Jaylen struggles with a skateboarding trick. Has there ever been an activity that you've had trouble learning? Write about it. What were you trying to do? How did you overcome your struggles?

3. Imagine you caught one of your friends trying to cheat off your test. What would you do?

4. Motivation means the desire to do something. Reread the story and look for Jess's motivation. Why do you think she cheats? Use examples from the story to explain your answer.

5. Read another Jess and Jaylen story, paying special attention to the things they do and say in that story. Are there things they say and do that are similar in each story? List the examples you find.

6. Mrs. Johnson makes Jess retake the two tests she cheated on. Do you think this was a fair punishment? Why or why not?

ABOUT THE AUTHOR

Blake Hoena grew up in central Wisconsin. In his youth, he wrote stories about robots conquering the moon and trolls lumbering around the woods behind his parents' house. Later, he moved to Minnesota to pursue a master of fine arts degree in creative writing from Minnesota State University, Mankato. He now lives in Saint Paul with his wife, two kids, a dog, and a couple of cats.

Blake has written more than 60 books for children—everything from ABC books about dogs to a series of graphic novels about two alien brothers bent on conquering Earth, chapter books about Batman and Superman, and retellings of classic stories such as *Treasure Island* and *Peter Pan*.

ABOUT THE ILLUSTRATOR

Dana Regan is originally from Lake Nebagamon, Wisconsin, and has her bachelor of fine arts degree in illustration from Washington University in Saint Louis, Missouri. She has illustrated more than 75 books and written seven early reader books, which, collectively, have sold more than 1 million copies. She lives and works in Kansas City, Missouri, with her sons, Joe and Tommy, who are a constant source of inspiration and tech support.